Richard Herne Shepherd

The bibliography of Thackeray a bibliographical list

Richard Herne Shepherd

The bibliography of Thackeray a bibliographical list

ISBN/EAN: 9783337221935

Printed in Europe, USA, Canada, Australia, Japan

Cover: Foto ©Raphael Reischuk / pixelio.de

More available books at **www.hansebooks.com**

THE

Bibliography of Thackeray

A BIBLIOGRAPHICAL LIST

ARRANGED IN CHRONOLOGICAL ORDER

OF THE

PUBLISHED WRITINGS IN PROSE AND VERSE
AND THE SKETCHES AND DRAWINGS

OF

WILLIAM MAKEPEACE THACKERAY

(FROM 1829 TO 1880)

A COMPANION AND SUPPLEMENT TO THE
EDITION DE LUXE

LONDON: ELLIOT STOCK 62 PATERNOSTER ROW E.C.

TO

JOSIAH TEMPLE

THIS LITTLE BIBLIOGRAPHY

IS AFFECTIONATELY AND GRATEFULLY

INSCRIBED

PREFACE.

A LARGE proportion of this little Bibliography is necessarily occupied with the enumeration of Thackeray's contributions to *Fraser's Magazine* and to *Punch*, both ranging over periods of ten years. As many of these are not reprinted in any edition of his Collected Works, I have endeavoured to make the list as complete as possible; and in the case of the contributions to *Fraser*, I have every reason to believe I have succeeded. But in the case of *Punch* (where, indeed, one is almost overwhelmed with the *embarras de richesses*), I have preferred rather to omit some items of minor interest than to run the risk of including anything doubtful. For although the well-known and familiar signature of the spectacles at once identifies any illustration as Thackeray's, it does not necessarily follow that the letter-press accompanying it was always his. But I have included everything that is reprinted in his Collected Works, and much that is not reprinted there.

As in my previous Bibliographies every article,

without exception, has been described with the actual book, pamphlet, magazine, or newspaper lying before me.

It should be added that the list of "Thackerayana" at the end makes no pretensions to be exhaustive.

I shall be happy to acknowledge and shall be grateful for any suggestions or additions that correspondents may obligingly communicate to me.

RICHARD HERNE SHEPHERD.

5, BRAMERTON-STREET,
    KING'S-ROAD, CHELSEA,
    November, 1880.

THE

BIBLIOGRAPHY OF THACKERAY.

1

THE SNOB: *A Literary and Scientific Journal, not " con-ducted by Members of the University."* Cambridge : Published by W. H. Smith, Rose-crescent. 1829, 12mo, pp. 64.

Consisting of eleven weekly numbers printed on paper of several different colours, commencing Thursday, April 9, and ending Thursday, June 18, 1829.

Among the contributions probably to be attributed to Thackeray are the mock-poem on Timbuctoo, and the continuation of Mrs. Ramsbottom's Letters.

2

Contributions in verse and prose to *The National Standard and Journal of Literature, Science, Music, Theatricals and the Fine Arts.* London : Thomas Hurst, 65, St. Paul's Churchyard. 1833, 4to.

The contributions distinctly traceable as Thackeray's are as follows :—

B

Vol. i.

No. 18, May 4, 1833, p. 273. Louis Philippe (Verses and Sketch).

No. 19, May 11, 1833, p. 289. Mr. Braham, [Mock] "Sonnet by W. Wordsworth," and Sketch.

No. 20, May 18, 1833, p. 305. N. M. Roths-child, Esq. (Verses and Sketch).

No. 22, June 1, 1833, p. 345. A. Bunn (Verses and Sketch).

No. 23, June 8, 1833, p. 362. Love in Fetters; a Tottenham-court-road Ditty (with Sketch).

No. 24, June 15, 1833, pp. 380-381. Covent Garden (with Sketch).

No. 25, June 22, 1833, p. 395. Petrus Laureus [Sir Peter Laurie], Verses and Sketch.

No. 26, June 29, 1833, pp. 412-413. Paris Correspondence (with Sketch).

Vol. ii.

No. 27, July 6, 1833, pp. 10-11. Paris Correspondence (with Sketch).

No. 28, July 13, 1833, pp. 28-29. Paris Correspondence (with Sketch).

No. 29, July 20, 1833, pp. 42-43. Paris Correspondence (with Sketch).

No. 32, August 10, 1833, pp. 85-86, and

No. 34, August 24, 1833,* pp. 121-122. The Devil's Wager (with an Illustration).

The Devil's Wager, with the same illustration reproduced in a somewhat altered form, is reprinted in *The Paris Sketch Book* (1840), vol. ii., pp. 83-101. There are some verbal alterations throughout, and the words of the incantation of Father Ignatius are omitted in the later version.

3

FLORE ET ZEPHYR. BALLET MYTHOLOGIQUE PAR THÉOPHILE WAGSTAFF. — London: Published March 1st, 1836, by J. Mitchell, Library, 33, Old Bond-street. A Paris, chez Rittner & Goupil, Boulevard Montmartre. Folio.

Eight plates, lithographed by Edward Morton, of which the following is the letterpress description :

1. La Danse fait ses offrandes sur l'autel de l'Harmonie.
2. Jeux Innocens de Zephyr et Flore.
3. Flore déplore l'absence de Zephyr.
4. Dans un pas-seul il exprime son extrême desespoir.
5. Triste et abattu, les séductions des Nymphes le tentent en vain.
6. Réconciliation de Flore et Zephyr.
7. La Retraite de Flore.
8. Les Délassements de Zephyr ; and vignette on wrapper-title.

* With this number Thackeray's contributions appear to have ceased, though the Journal itself continued to exist until February 1, 1834, completing a second volume and running on to a fragment (eighty pages) of a third.

4

THE YELLOWPLUSH CORRESPONDENCE. Fashionable Fax and Polite Annygoats. By Charles Yellowplush, Esq.—*Fraser's Magazine*, November, 1837 (vol. xvi., pp. 644-649).

A review of a volume entitled "My Book, or the Anatomy of Conduct," by a Mr. John Henry Skelton.

THE YELLOWPLUSH CORRESPONDENCE. No. II. Miss Shum's Husband.—January, 1838 (vol. xvii., pp. 39-49).

THE YELLOWPLUSH CORRESPONDENCE. No. III. Dimond cut Dimond.—February, 1838 (vol. xvii., pp. 243-250).

THE YELLOWPLUSH CORRESPONDENCE. No. IV. Skimmings from the Dairy of George IV.—March, 1838 (vol. xvii., pp. 353-359).

THE YELLOWPLUSH CORRESPONDENCE. No. V. Foring Parts.—April, 1838 (vol. xvii., pp. 404-408).

THE YELLOWPLUSH CORRESPONDENCE. No. VI. Mr. Deuceace at Paris.—May, 1838 (vol. xvii., pp. 616-627), and June, 1838 (vol. xvii., pp. 734-741).

THE YELLOWPLUSH CORRESPONDENCE. The End of

Mr. Deuceace's History.—July, 1838 (vol. xviii.,
pp. 59-71).

THE YELLOWPLUSH CORRESPONDENCE. Mr. Yellowplush's Ajew, August, 1838 (vol. xviii., pp. 195-
200).

5

Strictures on Pictures. A Letter from Michael Angelo
Titmarsh, Esq. — *Fraser's Magazine*, June, 1838
(vol. xvii., pp. 758-764).

With sketch by the author of " Titmarsh placing the laurel-
wreath on the brows of Mulready."

6

Twelve Plates illustrative of "Men of Character. By
Douglas Jerrold. In three volumes.— London :
Henry Colburn. 1838."

List of Plates : Vol. I. Practical Philosophy of Adam Buff ;
The Fall of Pippins ; Job Pippins a Murderer ; Jack Runnymede's
Dream. Vol. II. John Applejohn's Humane Intentions ; Maxi-
milian Tape before the "Lords ;" Final Reward of John Apple-
john. Vol. III. Barnaby Palms "feeling his way ;" Cheek's
Introduction to a new subject ; The Ghost of Kemp ; Matthew
Clear not "seeing his way ;" Introduction of Titus Trumps to
" Miss Wolfe."

"The illustrations were by Mr. W. M. Thackeray, now the
renowned novelist."—*Life and Remains of Douglas Jerrold, by
his son, Blanchard Jerrold.* London : 1859, p. 144.

7

THE "WHITEY-BROWN PAPER MAGAZINE." — Suggested to be issued in 1838-9, as a weekly publication.

A series of humorous sketches with brief descriptive letterpress, in prose and verse, representing the fortunes and misfortunes of Dionysius Diddler.

Facsimiled in the first eight numbers of *The Autographic Mirror*, February 20 to June 1, 1864 (vol. i., pp. 6, 15, 28, 39, 40, 60, 68, 76).

8

The Story of Mary Ancel.—Printed in *The New Monthly Magazine*. London : Colburn. October, 1838 (vol. liv., pp. 185-197).

Reprinted in the *Paris Sketch-Book* (vol. i., pp. 254-290).

9

SOME PASSAGES IN THE LIFE OF MAJOR GAHAGAN.— Printed in *The New Monthly Magazine*. London : Henry Colburn. February, March, November, December, 1838, and February, 1839 (vol. lii., pp. 174-182, 374-378 ; vol. liv., pp. 319-328, 543-552 ; vol. lv., pp. 266-281).

10

STUBBS'S CALENDAR; OR, THE FATAL BOOTS. With twelve illustrations by George Cruikshank.— Printed in *The Comic Almanack* for 1839. London: Charles Tilt.

11

CATHERINE: A STORY. By Ikey Solomons, Esq., junior.—*Fraser's Magazine*, May, June, July, August, November, 1839; and January and February, 1840.

With four full-page illustrations by the author: Mrs. Catharine's Temptation; The Interrupted Marriage; Captain Brock appears at Court with my Lord Peterborough; Catharine's Present to Mr. Hayes.

12

A Second Lecture on the Fine Arts, by Michael Angelo Titmarsh, Esq.—*Fraser's Magazine*, June, 1839 (vol. xix., pp. 743-750).

13

The French Plutarch, No. 1. 1. Cartouche. 2. Poinsinet.—*Fraser's Magazine*, October, 1839 (vol. xx., pp. 447-459).

Reprinted in the *Paris Sketch-Book*, 1840.

14

On the French School of Painting—in a Letter from Mr. Michael Angelo Titmarsh to Mr. MacGilp of London.—*Fraser's Magazine*, December, 1839 (vol. xx., pp. 679-688).

15

BARBER COX, AND THE CUTTING OF HIS COMB.   With twelve illustrations by George Cruikshank.—Printed in *The Comic Almanack* for 1840.   London : Charles Tilt.

Afterwards entitled " Cox's Diary."

16

Epistles to the Literati.   Ch-s Y-ll-wpl-sh, Esq., to Sir Edward Lytton Bulwer, Bart.   John Thomas Smith, Esq., to C—s Y—h, Esq.—*Fraser's Magazine*, January, 1840 (vol. xxi., pp. 71-80).

17

L'ABBAYE DE PENMARC'H, Mélodrame en trois actes, par MM. Tournemine et Thackeray.   Musique de M. Roger.   Décors de M. Desmarets, représenté

pour la première fois à Paris, sur le Théâtre de la
Porte-Saint-Antoine, le 1er février, 1840.—Paris :
Au Bureau Central, Rue d'Enghien, 1840, 8vo, pp.
21, in wrapper, printed in double columns.

This forms No. 53 of the "Répertoire Dramatique des
Auteurs Contemporains."

18

The Bedford-Row Conspiracy. In two Parts.—
Printed in *The New Monthly Magazine*, January,
March and April, 1840 (vol. lviii., pp. 99-111,
416-425, 547-557).

19

The Paris Sketch-Book. By Mr. Titmarsh.
With numerous designs by the author, on copper
and wood. In two volumes, pp. 304, 298.—
London : John Macrone, 1840.

CONTENTS OF VOL. I.

Contents of Vol. II.

The Preface is dated " London, July 1, 1840."

The Student's Quarter, or Paris Five-and-Thirty Years Since, by the late William Makepeace Thackeray. Not included in his Collected Writings. With original coloured illustrations. London : John Camden Hotten, Piccadilly (*n.d.*), pp. 202.

The eight chapters or letters of which this volume is composed were written by Thackeray during his residence in Paris in the year 1839. It is stated by the editor, who was also the publisher of the volume, that " they were originally addressed to a friend, the editor of a foreign journal, in whose publication they first appeared."

Of the eight Letters seven were reprinted in substance in the *Paris Sketch-Book* in 1840, with here and there a slight omission or alteration, hardly of sufficient interest to note. The only letter, therefore, "not included in Thackeray's ' Collected Writings ' is that which stands as the fifth, and is entitled ' More Aspects of Paris Life '" (pp. 113-132), and dated August 31.

The signature " T. T.," which is appended by the author to all of these letters but the eighth and last, had already been used by him three years previously in a series of letters of no permanent interest or value written by him from Paris as the correspondent of the *Constitutional*, a journal conducted by his stepfather. The last letter is signed " M. A. T.," which may be supposed to stand for " Michael Angelo Titmarsh," the author's favourite *nom-de-plume* for many years.

The name of the " foreign journal " in which these letters appeared was not furnished by the editor ; but he seems to hint in his memorial volume, "Thackeray the Humourist and the Man of Letters," that it was an American journal.

It should be added that the coloured illustrations which figure in this volume were not executed to accompany the letter-press, even if, as seems probable, they are rightly attributed to Thackeray's pencil.

20

GEORGE CRUIKSHANK.—Printed in *The Westminster Review*, June, 1840 (vol. xxxiv., pp. 1-60).

With numerous illustrations, printed from the original plates, or transferred to stone.

21

A Pictorial Rhapsody, by Michael Angelo Titmarsh. With an Introductory Letter to Mr. Yorke.— *Fraser's Magazine*, June 1840 (vol. xxi., pp. 720-732).
A Pictorial Rhapsody, concluded, and followed by a remarkable statement of facts by Mrs. Barbara.— *Fraser's Magazine*, July, 1840 (vol. xxii., pp. 112-126).

22

Going to see a Man Hanged. Signed W. M. T.— *Fraser's Magazine*, August, 1840 (vol. xxii., pp. 150-158.

23

A SHABBY GENTEEL STORY. In Nine Chapters.—
Fraser's Magazine, June, July, August, October,
1840.

When *A Shabby Genteel Story* was reprinted in the fourth
volume of Thackeray's *Miscellanies: Prose and Verse* (pp. 221-
324), a brief note of fourteen lines was added at the end, signed,
" W. M. T," and dated " London : April 10, 1857."

24

Captain Rook and Mr. Pigeon. By William Thacke-
ray. With two illustrations by Kenny Meadows.—
Printed in *Heads of the People: or, Portraits of the
English. Drawn by Kenny Meadows. With Original
Essays by distinguished writers.* London : Robert
Tyas, 50, Cheapside, 1840, pp. 305-320.

25

The Fashionable Authoress. By William Thackeray.
With an illustration by Kenny Meadows.—Printed
in *Heads of the People : or, Portraits of the English.
Drawn by Kenny Meadows. With Original Essays by
distinguished writers.* London : Robert Tyas, 1841,
pp. 73-84.

26

The Artist. By Michael Angelo Titmarsh. With an illustration by Kenny Meadows.—Printed in Kenny Meadows's *Heads of the People*. London : 1841, pp. 161-176.

These three contributions to Kenny Meadows's *Heads of the People* were reprinted at the end of the second volume of Thackeray's collected *Miscellanies* (London, 1856), pp. 443-494.

27

COMIC TALES AND SKETCHES. EDITED AND ILLUS-TRATED BY MR. MICHAEL ANGELO TITMARSH. In two volumes. London : Hugh Cunningham, 1841, 12mo (vol. i., pp. vii., 299 ; vol. ii., pp. 370).

The Preface is dated "Paris, April 1, 1841."

Contents of Vol. I. :—THE YELLOWPLUSH PAPERS.—1. Miss Shum's Husband ; 2. The Amours of Mr. Deuceace—Dimond cut Dimond ; 3. Skimmings from the Dairy of George IV. ; 4. Foring Parts ; 5. Mr. Deuceace at Paris, in ten chapters ; 6. Mr. Yellowplush's Ajew ; 7. Epistles to the Literati.

Contents of Vol. II. :—Some Passages in the Life of Major Gahagan ; The Professor ; The Bedford-Row Conspiracy ; Stubbs's Calendar, or the Fatal Boots.

28

THE SECOND FUNERAL OF NAPOLEON ; in Three Letters to Miss Smith, of London, and The

Chronicle of the Drum. By Mr. M. A. Titmarsh.
London : Hugh Cunningham. 1841, pp. 122.

With frontispiece of "Tomb in the Chapel of the Invalides,"
and vignette drawn by the author on the coloured wrapper.

At the end of this little work is advertised, as "preparing for
immediate publication, 'Dinner Reminiscences; or, The Young
Gormandiser's Guide at Paris.' By Mr. M. A. Titmarsh," to
be issued by the same publisher.

"The Second Funeral of Napoleon" was reprinted (with
prefatory note), from the original manuscript, in the *Cornhill
Magazine*, January, 1866 (vol. xiii., pp. 48-80). A small portion
of the manuscript is facsimiled in *The Autographic Mirror*,
No. 1, Saturday, February 20, 1864 (vol. i., p. 6).

29

Memorials of Gormandising. In a letter to Oliver
Yorke, Esq., by M. A. Titmarsh.—*Fraser's Magazine*,
June, 1841 (vol. xxiii., pp. 710-725).

30

On Men and Pictures. Apropos of a Walk in the
Louvre.—*Fraser's Magazine*, July, 1841 (vol. xxiv.,
pp. 98-111).

31

Men and Coats.—*Fraser's Magazine*, August, 1841
(vol. xxiv., pp. 208-217).

32

THE HISTORY OF SAMUEL TITMARSH AND THE
GREAT HOGGARTY DIAMOND. Edited and illus-
trated by Sam's Cousin, Michael Angelo.—*Fraser's
Magazine*, September, October, November and
December, 1841 (vol. xxiv.).

33

Dickens in France (with two illustrations by the
author).—*Fraser's Magazine*, March, 1842 (vol.
xxv., pp. 342-352).

An account of a French dramatic version of "Nicholas
Nickleby," performed at a Paris theatre.

34

Little Spitz. A Lenten Anecdote, from the German
of Professor Spass. By Michael Angelo Titmarsh.
With woodcut illustration by George Cruikshank.—
Printed in *George Cruikshank's Omnibus*, edited by
Laman Blanchard. London : Tilt and Bogue.
1842, pp. 167-172.

35

The King of Brentford's Testament. By Michael
Angelo Titmarsh.—Printed in *George Cruikshank's
Omnibus*. 1842, pp. 244-246.

36

FITZ-BOODLE'S CONFESSIONS. — *Fraser's Magazine*, June, 1842 (vol. xxv., pp. 707-721).

PROFESSIONS BY GEORGE FITZ-BOODLE. Being appeals to the unemployed younger sons of the nobility.—*Fraser's Magazine*, July, 1842 (vol. xxvi., pp. 43-60).

FITZ-BOODLE'S CONFESSIONS. Miss Löwe.—*Fraser's Magazine*, October, 1842 (vol. xxvi., pp. 395-405).

CONFESSIONS OF GEORGE FITZ-BOODLE. Dorothea. —*Fraser's Magazine*, January, 1843 (vol. xxvii., pp. 76-84).

CONFESSIONS OF GEORGE FITZ-BOODLE. Ottilia.— *Fraser's Magazine*, February, 1843 (vol. xxvii., pp. 214-224).

CONFESSIONS OF GEORGE FITZ-BOODLE. Men's Wives. Mr. and Mrs. Frank Berry.—*Fraser's Magazine*, March, 1843 (vol. xxvii., pp. 349-361).

With an illustration by the author.

37

THE IRISH SKETCH-BOOK. BY MR. M. A. TITMARSH. With numerous engravings on wood, drawn by the author. In two volumes, 12mo. London:

Chapman and Hall, 186, Strand, 1843.   (Vol. i.,
pp. vi. 311 ; vol. ii., pp. vi. 327).

The Dedication, to Dr. Charles Lever, is dated "London,
April 27, 1843."

38

CONFESSIONS OF GEORGE FITZ-BOODLE.   Men's
Wives, No. II.   The Ravenswing.   In eight Chapters.—*Fraser's Magazine*, April to June, August,
and September, 1843.

39

Jerome Paturot.   With Considerations on Novels in
General.   In a letter from M. A. Titmarsh.—
Fraser's Magazine, September, 1843 (vol. xxviii.,
pp. 349-362).

40

Bluebeard's Ghost.   By M. A. Titmarsh.—*Fraser's
Magazine*, October, 1843 (vol. xxviii., pp. 413-425).

41

MEN'S WIVES.   BY GEORGE FITZ-BOODLE.   No. III.
Dennis Haggarty's Wife.—*Fraser's Magazine*, Oc-
tober, 1843 (vol. xxviii., pp. 494-504).
MEN'S WIVES.   BY GEORGE FITZ-BOODLE.   No. IV.
The ——'s Wife.—*Fraser's Magazine*, November,
1843 (vol. xxviii., pp. 581-592).

C

42

Grant in Paris.   By Fitz Boodle.—*Fraser's Magazine*, December, 1843 (vol. xxviii., pp. 702-712).

A satirical notice of a book by Mr. James Grant, entitled "Paris and its People."

43

THE LUCK OF BARRY LYNDON.   A Romance of the Last Century.   By Fitz-Boodle.—*Fraser's Magazine*, January to September, November and December, 1844 (vols. xxix. and xxx.).

44

A Box of Novels.—*Fraser's Magazine*, February, 1844 (vol. xxix., pp. 153-169).

This article closes with the famous notice of Dickens's "Christmas Carol."

45.

THE HISTORY OF THE NEXT FRENCH REVOLUTION. (From a forthcoming History of Europe.)—*Punch*, February 24; March 2 to 30; April 6 to 20, 1844 (vol. vi.).   With fourteen illustrations.

Reprinted in Vol. XV. of Thackeray's Collected Works in twenty-four volumes.   London : 1879, pp. 163-201.

46

TITMARSH'S CARMEN LILLIENSE.—*Fraser's Magazine*, March, 1844 (vol. xxix., pp. 361-363).

47

Review of "A New Spirit of the Age, edited by R. H. Horne." *Morning Chronicle*, Tuesday, April 2, 1844, p. 6.

This notice is referred to and quoted as the work of Mr. Michael Angelo Titmarsh in Mr. Horne's Introductory Comments to the second edition of his "New Spirit of the Age."

48

LITTLE TRAVELS AND ROAD-SIDE SKETCHES. By TITMARSH. (From Richmond in Surrey to Brussels in Belgium.)—*Fraser's Magazine*, May, 1844 (vol. xxix., pp. 517-528).

49

May Gambols; or, Titmarsh in the Picture Galleries.— *Fraser's Magazine*, June, 1844 (vol. xxix., pp. 700-716).

50

CONTRIBUTIONS TO THE NEW MONTHLY MAGAZINE. London: Henry Colburn. 1844.

Vol. lxxi.

May, 1844. The Partie Fine, by Lancelot Wagstaff, Esq., pp. 22-28.

June, 1844. Arabella; or, the Moral of "The
Partie Fine" (signed TITMARSH), pp. 169-
172.

July, 1844. Greenwich—Whitebait. By Mr.
Wagstaff, pp. 416-421.

51

Wanderings of our Fat Contributor. *Punch*, August
3, 1844 (vol. vii., pp. 61-62).

With three illustrations by the author.

TRAVELLING NOTES BY OUR FAT CONTRIBUTOR.
Punch, August 10, 1844 (vol. vii., pp. 66-67).

With an illustration by the author.

August 17, 1844 (vol. vii., pp. 83-84).

With three illustrations by the author.

November 30, 1844 (vol. vii., p. 237).

With two illustrations by the author.

December 7, 1844 (vol. vii., pp. 256-257).

With three illustrations by the author.

December 14, 1844 (vol. vii., pp. 265-266).

With four illustrations by the author.

52

LITTLE TRAVELS AND ROAD-SIDE SKETCHES. By
Titmarsh. No. II. Ghent—Bruges.—*Fraser's Magazine*, October, 1844 (vol. xxx., pp. 465-471). No.
III. Waterloo.—*Fraser's Magazine*, January, 1845
(vol. xxxi., pp. 94-96).

53

PUNCH IN THE EAST.   FROM OUR FAT CONTRIBU-
TOR.—*Punch*, January 11, 1845 (vol. viii., pp. 31-
32).

> With an illustration by the author.

January 18, 1845 (vol. viii., pp. 35-36).

> With two illustrations by the author.

January 25, 1845 (vol. viii., p. 45).

> With three illustrations by the author.

February 1, 1845 (vol. viii., p. 61).

> With two illustrations by the author.

February 8, 1845 (vol. viii., p. 75).

> With an illustration by the author.

54

Picture Gossip: in a Letter from Michael Angelo
Titmarsh.—*Fraser's Magazine*, June, 1845 (vol.
xxxi., pp. 713-724).

55

CONTRIBUTIONS TO THE NEW MONTHLY MAGAZINE.
London : Colburn. (*Continued*)

Vol. lxxiv.

July, 1845. The Chest of Cigars. By Lancelot
Wagstaff, Esq., pp. 381-385.
August, 1845. Bob Robinson's First Love. By
Lancelot Wagstaff, Esq., pp. 519-525.

56

The Pimlico Pavilion. By the Mulligan (of Kilbally-
mulligan).—*Punch*, August 9, 1845 (vol. ix., p. 66).

57

Meditations on Solitude. By our Stout Commissioner.
Punch, September 13, 1845 (vol. ix., p. 123).

With an illustration by the author.

58

Beulah Spa. By "Punch's" Commissioner.—*Punch*,
September 27, 1845 (vol. ix., pp. 137-138).

With two illustrations by the author.

59

The Georges.—*Punch*, October 11, 1845 (vol. ix., p.
159).

60

A LEGEND OF THE RHINE. BY MICHAEL ANGELO
TITMARSH. With fourteen woodcut illustrations
by George Cruikshank.—Printed in *George Cruikshank's Table-Book, edited by Gilbert Abbott à Beckett.*
London : Published at the *Punch* Office, 1845.

Divided into thirteen chapters ; published in instalments,
commencing in the sixth and ending in the twelfth and last
number.

61

Notice of N. P. Willis's *Dashes at Life.*—Printed in
the *Edinburgh Review*, October, 1845 (vol. lxxxii.,
pp. 470-480).

62

Two letters to Macvey Napier, Esq., Editor of the
Edinburgh Review, dated "St. James's-street, July

16, 1845," and "October 16, 1845," and signed
"W. M. Thackeray."—Printed in *Selection from the
Correspondence of the late Macvey Napier*, edited by
his son.   London : Macmillan & Co., 1879, pp.
498-499.

63

Barmecide Banquets with Joseph Bregion and Anne
   Miller.   George Savage Fitz-Boodle, Esquire, to the
   Rev. Lionel Gaster.—*Fraser's Magazine*, November,
   1845 (vol. xxxii., pp. 584-593).

64

Brighton.   By   "Punch's   Commissioner."—*Punch*,
   October 11, 1845 (vol. ix., p. 158).

> With three illustrations by the author.

A Brighton Night Entertainment.   By "Punch's
   Commissioner."—*Punch*, October 18, 1845 (vol. ix.,
   p. 168).

> With four illustrations by the author.

Meditations over Brighton.   By "Punch's" Commissioner."   (From the Devil's Dyke.)—*Punch*,
   October 25, 1845 (vol. ix., p. 187).

> With an illustration by the author.

65

A Doe in the City. By Frederick Haltamont de Montmorency.—*Punch*, November 1, 1845 (vol. ix., p. 191).

> With an illustration by the author.

66

About a Christmas Book. In a Letter from Michael Angelo Titmarsh to Oliver Yorke, Esq.—*Fraser's Magazine*, December, 1845 (vol. xxxii., pp. 744-748).

> A notice of " Poems and Pictures : A Collection of Ballads, Songs, and other Poems. With designs on wood by the principal artists ; 4to. London : James Burns, 1845."

67

A Lucky Speculator. (With " Jeames of Buckley Square, A Heligy ").—*Punch*, August 2, 1845 (vol. ix., p. 59).

> With an illustration by John Leech.

A Letter from " Jeames of Buckley Square."—*Punch*. August 16, 1845 (vol. ix., p. 76).

Jeames on Time Bargings.—*Punch*, November 1, 1845 (vol. ix., p. 195).

> With an illustration.

Jeames's Diary.—*Punch*, November 8 to 29 ; December 6, 13, 1845 (vol. ix.) ; December 27, 1845 ; January 3, 10, 17, 31; February 7, 1846 (vol. x.).

With twenty illustrations by the author.

68

Notes of a Journey from Cornhill to Grand Cairo, by way of Lisbon, Athens, Constantinople and Jerusalem. Performed in the Steamers of the Peninsular and Oriental Company. By Mr. M. A. Titmarsh. London : Chapman and Hall, 186, Strand. 1846.

With coloured frontispiece and numerous woodcut illustrations by the author. The Dedication, to Captain Samuel Lewis, is dated " London : December 24, 1845."

69

Ronsard to his Mistress. Signed "Michael Angelo Titmarsh."—*Fraser's Magazine*, January, 1846 (vol. xxxiii., p. 120).

70

A Brother of the Press on the History of a Literary Man, Laman Blanchard, and the chances of the Literary Profession. In a Letter to the Reverend Francis Sylvester at Rome, from Michael Angelo Titmarsh, Esq.—*Fraser's Magazine*, March, 1846 (vol. xxxiii., pp. 332-342).

71

Titmarsh *v.* Tait. Letter to Mr. Punch. Signed
"Michael Angelo Titmarsh," and dated "Blue
Posts, March 10, 1846."—*Punch*, March 14, 1846
(vol. x., p. 124).

72

On some Illustrated Children's Books. By Michael
Angelo Titmarsh.—*Fraser's Magazine*, April, 1846
(vol. xxxiii., pp. 495-502).

73

Jeames on the Gauge Question.—*Punch*, May 16,
1846 (vol. x., p. 223). With an illustration.
Mr. Jeames again.—*Punch*, June 13, 1846 (vol. x.,
p. 267).

With an illustration by the author.

74

Proposals for a Continuation of Ivanhoe. In a letter
to Monsieur Alexandre Dumas, by Monsieur
Michael Angelo Titmarsh. — *Fraser's Magazine*,
August and September, 1846 (vol. xxxiv., pp. 237-
245, 359-367).

75

MRS. PERKINS'S BALL.   BY MR. M. A. TITMARSH.—
London : Chapman and Hall, 186, Strand.   1847,
pp. 46.

With illustrations by the author, coloured in some of the
copies.

76

THE SNOBS OF ENGLAND.   BY ONE OF THEMSELVES.

With numerous illustrations by the author. Commencing
in *Punch* of February 28, 1846 (vol. x., p. 101), and ending
February 27, 1847 (vol. xii., p. 86). (Prefatory Remarks and
fifty-two Chapters.)

THE BOOK OF SNOBS : BY W. M. THACKERAY. London :
Punch Office, 1848, pp. viii. 180, in green wrapper (with all the
original illustrations and a vignette on title, not appearing in the
Punch issue).

The following Chapters are omitted in the Collected Edition :
Chapter XVII. On Literary Snobs, in a letter from " One of
themselves " to Mr. Smith, the celebrated penny-a-liner (*Punch*,
June 27, 1846, vol. x., p. 281); Chapter XVIII. On some Politi-
cal Snobs (*Punch*, July 4, 1846, vol. xi., p. 4) ; Chapter XIX.
On Whig Snobs (July 11, 1846, vol. xi., p. 19 ; Chapter XX.
On Conservative or Country-Party Snobs (July 18, 1846, vol. xi.,
p. 23) ; Chapter XXI. Are there any Whig Snobs? (July 25,
1846, vol. xi., p. 39) ; Chapter XXII. On the Snob Civilian
(August 1, 1846, vol. xi., p. 43) ; Chapter XXIII. On Radical
Snobs (August 8, 1846, vol. xi., p. 59).

"On reperusing these papers," says the author, p. 66, *note*,
" I have found them so stupid, so personal, so snobbish—in a
word—that I have withdrawn them from this collection."

77

A Grumble about the Christmas Books.   By Michael Angelo Titmarsh. — *Fraser's Magazine*, January, 1847 (vol. xxxv., pp. 111-126).

Among the books noticed is Charles Dickens's "Battle of Life : A Love-Story."

78

VANITY FAIR. A NOVEL WITHOUT A HERO. BY WILLIAM MAKEPEACE THACKERAY. With Illustrations on Steel and Wood by the Author.— London : Bradbury and Evans.   1848, pp. xvi., 624.

Issued in monthly instalments in yellow wrappers, originally bearing the title "Vanity Fair : Pen and Pencil Sketches o English Society.   By W. M. Thackeray."   On the wrapper is an illustration by the author not reproduced in the body of the work.   No. 1 is dated January, 1847, and Nos. 19 and 20 (double number), July, 1848.
    The Preface ("Before the Curtain ") is dated "London : June 28, 1848."

79

An Eastern Adventure of the Fat Contributor.— *Punch's Pocket Book*, for 1847, pp. 148-156.

With full-page illustration by the author.

80

The Mahogany Tree.—*Punch*, January 9, 1847 (vol. xii., p. 13).

The second stanza is omitted in Thackeray's Collected Ballads. (*Miscellanies*, vol. i. (1855), pp. 47-48).

81

Two Letters to William Edmondstoune Aytoun, dated " 13, Young Street, Kensington, January 2," and "January 13, 1847," and signed "W. M. Thackeray."—Printed in *Memoir of William Edmondstoune Aytoun*, by Theodore Martin. Blackwood and Sons, Edinburgh and London, 1867, pp. 131-135.

82

Mr. Jeames's Sentiments on the Cambridge Election. —*Punch*, March 6, 1847 (vol. xii., p. 102).

83

Love-Songs made Easy. " What makes my heart to thrill and glow ?" Song by Fitzroy Clarence.— *Punch*, March 6, 1847 (vol. xii., p. 101).

With an illustration by the author.

Love-Songs by the Fat Contributor.   The Domestic Love-Song.   "The Cane-Bottomed Chair."
—*Punch*, March 27, 1847 (vol. xii., p. 125).

> With two illustrations by the author.

Love-Songs of the Fat Contributor.   The Ghazul, or Oriental Love-Song.   The Rocks.   The Merry Bard.   The Caïque.—*Punch*, June 5, 1847 (vol. xii., p. 227).

> With two illustrations by the author.

84

Punch's Prize Novelists :

1. George de Barnwell.—*Punch*, April 3-17, 1847.

> With three illustrations by the author.

2. Codlingsby.   By B. de Shrewsbury, Esq.—*Punch*, April 24, May 15 to 29, 1847.

> With four illustrations by the author.

3. Lords and Liveries.—*Punch*, June 12 to 26, 1847.

> With three illustrations by the author.

4. Barbazure.   By G. P. R. Jeames, Esq.—*Punch*, July 10 to 24, 1847.

> With five illustrations by the author.

5. Phil. Fogarty. A Tale of the Fighting Onety-
Oneth. By Harry Rollicker.—*Punch*, August
7 to 21, 1847.

   With five illustrations by the author.

6. Crinoline.   By   Je-mes   Pl-sh,   Esq.—*Punch*,
August 28, September 4, 11, 1847.

   With six illustrations by the author.

7. The Stars and Stripes.—*Punch*, September 25,
October 9, 1847.

   With two illustrations by the author.

85

Brighton in 1847. By the F. C.
Punch, October 23, 1847 (vol. xiii., p. 153); October
30, 1847 (vol. xiii., pp. 157-158).

   With three illustrations by the author.

86

TRAVELS IN LONDON, by SPEC.   *Punch*, November
20, 1847 (vol. xiii., p. 193).

   With an illustration.

TRAVELS IN LONDON. The Curate's Walk. November 27, 1847.

   With nine illustrations by the author.

TRAVELS IN LONDON. A Walk with the Curate.
December 4, 1847. A Dinner in the City. December
11, 25, and 31, 1847.

TRAVELS IN LONDON. A Night's Pleasure.—*Punch*,
January 8-29 and February 12, 19, 1848. (With
ten illustrations by the author.) A Club in an
Uproar.—*Punch*, March 11, 1848 (vol. xiv., pp.
95-96). With two illustrations by the author. A
Roundabout Ride.—*Punch*, March 25, 1848 (vol.
xiv., p. 119). With an illustration by the author.

87

'OUR STREET." BY MR. M. A. TITMARSH. London :
Chapman and Hall, 186, Strand. 1848, pp. 54.

With illustrations by the author, coloured in some of the
copies.

88

The Persecution of British Footmen. By Mr. Jeames.
—*Punch*, April 1 and 8, 1848 (vol. xiv., pp. 131,
143-144).

With three illustrations.

89

The Battle of Limerick.—*Punch*, May 13, 1848 (vol.
xiv., p. 195).

D

90

On the New Forward Movement.   A Letter from our old friend, Mr. Snob, to Mr. Joseph Hume.—*Punch*, May 20, 1848 (vol. xiv., p. 207).

With an illustration.

91

Mr. Snob's Remonstrance with Mr. Smith.—*Punch*, May 27, 1848 (vol. xiv., p. 217).

With an illustration.

92

A LITTLE DINNER AT TIMMINS'S.—*Punch*, May 27; June 17 and 24, and July 1, 8, 22 and 29, 1848 (vol. xiv., pp. 219-223, 247, 258; vol. xv., pp. 5, 13, 33-34, 43).

With eight illustrations by the author.

93

Letters to a Nobleman visiting Ireland.—*Punch*, September 2-9, 1848 (vol. xv., pp. 95-96, 107).

With two illustrations by the author.

94

Science at Cambridge.—*Punch*, November 11, 1848 (vol. xv., p. 201).

With an illustration.

95

A Bow Street Ballad. By a Gentleman of the Force (Signed "Policeman X. 54").—*Punch*, November 25, 1848 (vol. xv., p. 229).

With an illustration.

96

Death of the Earl of Robinson. (In the manner of a popular Necrographer.)—*Punch*, December 2, 1848 (vol. xv., p. 231).

With an illustration.

97

Bow Street Ballads. No. II. Jacob Omnium's Hoss. *Punch*, December 9, 1848 (vol. xv., p. 251).

With an illustration.

98

An Interesting Event.   By Mr. Titmarsh.—Printed in
The Keepsake, 1849, *edited by the Countess of Blessing-
ton.*   London : David Bogue.   1849, pp. 207-215.

99

THE HISTORY OF PENDENNIS ; HIS FORTUNES AND
MISFORTUNES, HIS FRIENDS AND HIS GREATEST
ENEMY.   BY WILLIAM MAKEPEACE THACKERAY.
With illustrations on steel and wood by the
Author.   In two volumes (pp. viii. 384, xii. 372).
London : Bradbury and Evans, 1849-50.

Originally issued in monthly numbers in yellow wrappers,
No 1 being dated November, 1848, and Nos. 23 and 24 (double
number) December, 1850.   After the appearance of the eleventh
number (dated September, 1849), the publication was suspended
during four months, on account of the author's illness.   The
twelfth number bears date January, 1850.   The Preface is dated
" Kensington, November 26th, 1850."

100

The Great Squattleborough Soirée.—*Punch*, December
16, 1848 (vol. xv., pp. 253-254).

With an illustration by the author, representing Dr. Johnson
and Boswell walking together.

101

The Three Christmas Waits.—*Punch*, December 23,
1848 (vol. xv., p. 265).

102

DOCTOR BIRCH AND HIS YOUNG FRIENDS. BY MR. M. A. TITMARSH. London: Chapman and Hall, 186, Strand. 1849, pp. 49.

With vignette title and fifteen full-page illustrations by the author, coloured in some of the copies. The "Epilogue" is in verse.

103

Child's Parties; and a Remonstrance concerning them.—*Punch*, January 13 and 27, 1849 (vol. xvi., pp. 13-14, 35-36).

With two illustrations by the author.

104

THE HISTORY OF SAMUEL TITMARSH AND THE GREAT HOGGARTY DIAMOND. BY W. M. THACKERAY.— London: Bradbury and Evans, 11, Bouverie-street. 1849, pp. xii., 189.

With engraved title and nine full-page illustrations by the author. The Preface is dated, "Kensington, January 25, 1849." The story appeared originally in *Fraser's Magazine* in the year 1841. *Vide supra*, p. 15, § 32.

105

Paris Revisited. By an Old Paris Man.—*Punch*, February 10, 1849 (vol. xvi., pp. 55-56).

With an illustration.

106

THE BALLAD OF BOUILLABAISSE. From the Contributor at Paris.—*Punch*, February 17, 1849 (vol. xvi., p. 67).

107

Two or Three Theatres at Paris.—*Punch*, February 24, 1849 (vol. xvi., p. 75).

With an illustration by Richard Doyle.

108

On Some Dinners at Paris.—*Punch*, March 3, 1849 (vol. xvi., p. 92).

With an illustration by Richard Doyle.

109

MR. BROWN'S LETTERS TO A YOUNG MAN ABOUT TOWN.

Introductory.—*Punch*, March 24, 1849 (vol. xvi., p. 115).

On Tailoring and Toilettes in General.—March 31, 1849, p. 125.

The Influence of Lovely Woman upon Society.—April 7, 1849, pp. 135-6.

Some More Words about the Ladies.—April 14, 1849, pp. 145-6.

On Friendship.—April 28, 1849, pp. 165-6; May 5, 1849, pp. 184-5.

Mr. Brown the Elder takes Mr. Brown the Younger to a Club.—May 12 to 26, 1849, pp. 187-8, 197-8, 207-8.

A Word about Balls in Season.—June 9, 1849, pp. 229-230.

A Word about Dinners.—June 16, 1849, pp. 239-240,

On some Old Customs of the Dinner-table.—June 23, 1849, pp. 249-250.

Great and Little Dinners.—July 7, 1849 (vol. xvii., pp. 1-2).

On Love, Marriage, Men, and Women.— July 14, 1849, pp. 13-14; July 21, 1849, p. 23; August 4, 1849, p. 43.

Out of Town.—August 11 and 18, 1849, pp. 53, 66-69.

With sixteen illustrations.

110

THE THREE SAILORS. (With Reminiscences of Michael Angelo Titmarsh at Rome.)—Printed in *Sand and Canvas; a Narrative of Adventures in Egypt, with a Sojourn among the Artists in Rome*, by Samuel Bevan. London : Charles Gilpin, 5, Bishopsgate-street-without, 1849, pp. 336-342.

THE THREE SAILORS. Autograph copy sent to Bevan (with note commencing " Dear Bevan," and signed " W. M. Thackeray ") for insertion in *Sand and Canvas.*—Facsimiled in *The Autographic Mirror*, No. 19, November 1, 1864 (vol. ii., p. 156).

In the *North British Review*, February, 1864 (vol. xl., p. 254), there is a printed version of "The Three Sailors," differing considerably from the above.

THE THREE SAILORS, by the late W. M. Thackeray (Sketch and Anecdote).—*The Editor's Box, A Midsummer Annual.* London : Cecil Brooks and Co., Strand, 1880, p. 80.

An exact reproduction in facsimile of a page from the autograph album of the late Shirley Brooks.

111

REBECCA AND ROWENA : A ROMANCE UPON ROMANCE. BY MR. M. A. TITMARSH. With illustrations by Richard Doyle. London : Chapman and Hall, 186, Strand. 1850, pp. viii. 102.

The Preface is dated "Kensington, December 20th, 1849." In some copies the full-page illustrations are coloured.

The substance of this story appeared in *Fraser's Magazine* for August and September, 1846. *Vide supra*, p. 27, § 74.

112

The Dignity of Literature. To the Editor of the *Morning Chronicle.* Letter of nearly a column and a half, dated "Reform Club, Jan. 8," and signed "W. M. Thackeray."—Printed in the *Morning Chronicle*, Saturday, January 12, 1850.

In answer to some remarks in a leading article which had appeared in the *Morning Chronicle* of Thursday, January 3.

113

Sketches after English Landscape Painters. By Louis Marvy. With short notices by W. M. Thackeray. London: David Bogue, 86, Fleet-street. 4to. [1850].

The letter-press consists of a Preface and twenty short notices of Sir A. W. Callcott, Turner, Holland, Danby, Creswick, Collins, Redgrave, Lee, Cattermole, W. J. Müller, Harding, Nasmyth, Richard Wilson, E. W. Cooke, John Constable, P. de Wint, Cox, Gainsborough, Roberts and Stanfield. There is no pagination to the volume.

114

Capers and Anchovies. To the Editor of the *Morning Chronicle*. Letter of nearly a column, dated "Garrick Club, April 11, 1850," and signed "Wm. Thackeray."—*Morning Chronicle*, Friday, April 12, 1850.

115

THE KICKLEBURYS ON THE RHINE. By Mr. M. A. TITMARSH. Second Edition. With Preface, being an Essay on Thunder and Small Beer. London: Smith, Elder and Co. 1851, pp. xv. 87.

With fifteen illustrations by the author, coloured in some of the copies.

116

MAY DAY ODE, containing 19 stanzas of 8 lines each, dated "April 29," and signed "W. M. Thackeray." Printed in the *Times*, Wednesday, April 30, 1851.

117

THE HISTORY OF HENRY ESMOND, ESQ., a Colonel in the service of Her Majesty Q. Anne. Written by himself. In Three Volumes. London : printed for Smith, Elder and Company, over against St. Peter's Church in Cornhill. 1852, pp. 344, vi. 319, vi. 324.

The half-title runs as follows :—"ESMOND : A STORY OF QUEEN ANNE'S REIGN. BY W. M. THACKERAY."

118

THE ENGLISH HUMOURISTS OF THE EIGHTEENTH CENTURY. A Series of Lectures delivered in England, Scotland, and the United States of America. By W. M. Thackeray. Second Edition, Revised. London : Smith, Elder, and Co. 1853, pp. 322.

119

Mr. Thackeray in the United States. To the Editor of *Fraser's Magazine.*—*F. M.*, January, 1853 (vol. xlvii., pp. 100-103). Signed "John Small."

120

Author's Preface to a Selection from his Contributions to *Punch*, published in America. 1. Mr. Brown's Letters to a Young Man about Town; with The Proser and other Papers. 2. Punch's Prize Novelists, The Fat Contributor, and Travels in London. By W. M. Thackeray. Two volumes. New York: D. Appleton and Co. 1853, pp. 256, 306.

This selection was made by the author himself during his first visit to America. The Preface, five pages, is signed " W. M. Thackeray," and dated " New York : December, 1852."

The Proser contains the following papers. 1. On a Lady in an Opera Box ; 2. On the pleasures of being a Fogy ; 3. On the benefits of being a Fogy.

The Miscellanies that follow comprise : 1. Child's Parties, and a Remonstrance concerning them ; 2. The Story of Koompanee Jehan ; 3. Science at Cambridge ; 4. A Dream of Whitefriars ; 5. Mr. Punch's Address to the Great City of Castlebar ; 6. Irish Gems ; 7. The Charles the Second Ball ; 8. The Georges ; 9. Death of the Earl of Robinson.

121

THE NEWCOMES. MEMOIRS OF A MOST RESPECTABLE FAMILY. EDITED BY ARTHUR PENDENNIS, ESQ. With illustrations on steel and wood, by Richard Doyle (vol. i., pp. viii. 380 ; vol. ii., pp. viii. 375). London : Bradbury and Evans, 11, Bouverie-street. 1854-1855.

Issued in twenty-four monthly numbers in yellow wrappers ; the first dated October, 1853, and the last (Nos. 23 and 24—a double number), August, 1855. The last chapter is dated at the end, "Paris, 28th June, 1855."

122

"Mr. Washington." To the Editor of the *Times*. Letter dated "Athenæum, Nov. 22," and signed "W. M. Thackeray."—*Times*, Wednesday, November 23, 1853.

In answer to some strictures of the New York Correspondent of the *Times* (dated "New York, Nov. 8," and printed in the *Times* of Nov. 22, 1853), respecting a passage in the first number of *The Newcomes*, which had given offence in the United States.

123

Lucy's Birthday,

"Seventeen rosebuds in a ring."

Three stanzas of eight lines each, dated "New York, April 15." Printed in *The Keepsake*, 1854, *edited by Miss Power.* London : David Bogue. 1854, p. 18.

124

LETTERS FROM THE EAST BY OUR OWN BASHI-BOZOUK.—*Punch*, June 24, July 1, 1854 (vol. xxvi., pp. 257-258, 267-268); July 8 to 29, August 5, 1854 (vol. xxvii., pp. 1-2, 11-12, 21-22, 31-32, 41).

With seven illustrations by the author.

125

Pictures of Life and Character. By John Leech.—
Quarterly Review, December, 1851 (vol. xcvi., pp.
75-86).

126

THE ROSE AND THE RING; or, the History of Prince
Giglio and Prince Bulbo. A Fire-side Pantomime
for Great and Small Children. By Mr. M. A.
Titmarsh. London : Smith, Elder, and Co., 65,
Cornhill. 1855, pp. iv. 128.

With illustrations by the author, plain in all the copies
The Preface, or "Prelude," is dated "December, 1854."

127

Reminiscences of Weimar and Goethe, in a letter
addressed to G. H. Lewes, dated "London, 28th
April, 1855," and signed "W. M. Thackeray."—
Printed in *Lewes's Life and Works of Goethe*,
London : David Nutt. 1855, vol. ii., pp. 442-446.

128

Address to the Electors of Oxford, dated "Mitre,
July 9, 1857," and signed "W. M. Thackeray."

129

Mr. Thackeray, Mr. Yates, and the Garrick Club.
The Correspondence and Facts. Stated by Edmund
Yates.—Printed for Private Circulation. 1859,
pp. 15.

Contains a letter to Mr. Edmund Yates, dated "36, Onslow-
square, June 14," and signed "W. M. Thackeray;" a letter to
the Committee of the Garrick Club, dated "36, Onslow-square,
June 19, 1858," signed "W. M. Thackeray;" a letter to Charles
Dickens, dated "36, Onslow-square, 26th November, 1858;"
and a letter to the Committee of the Garrick Club, dated
"Onslow-square, November 28, 1858," both signed "W. M.
Thackeray."

130

THE VIRGINIANS : A TALE OF THE LAST CENTURY.
BY W. M. THACKERAY. With illustrations on
steel and wood by the Author. In Two Volumes
(pp. viii. 382, viii. 376). London : Bradbury and
Evans. 1858-1859.

Issued in twenty-four monthly numbers (in yellow illustrated
wrapper), commencing November, 1857, and ending October,
1859.

131

Nil Nisi Bonum.—*Cornhill Magazine*, February, 1860
(vol. i., pp. 129-134).

132

The Last Sketch. (A short paper signed W. M. T.,
prefixed to " Emma, a Fragment of a Story by the
late Charlotte Brontë.")—*Cornhill Magazine*, April,
1860 (vol. i., pp. 485-487).

133

Vanitas Vanitatum. (Sixteen stanzas of four lines
each.)—*Cornhill Magazine*, July, 1860 (vol. ii., pp.
59-60).

134

A Leaf out of a Sketch-Book. By W. M. Thackeray.
—Printed in *The Victoria Regia, a Volume of
Original Contributions in Poetry and Prose, edited by
Adelaide A. Procter*. London : Emily Faithfull and
Co. 1861, pp. 118-125.

With two sketches by the author.

135

Lovel the Widower. By W. M. Thackeray.
With illustrations. London : Smith, Elder and
Co. 1861, pp. 258.

Originally published in monthly instalments in the first six
numbers of the *Cornhill Magazine* (January to June, 1860).

"The Wolves and the Lamb," the original of the story of *Lovel the Widower* (which was printed for the first time in the twenty-fourth and last volume of Thackeray's collected Works, London: Smith, Elder and Co., 1879, pp. 125-175), was written for the stage, and refused by the management of the Olympic about 1854.

136

THE FOUR GEORGES. BY W. M. THACKERAY. With illustrations. London: Smith, Elder, and Co. 1861, pp. 226.

> Originally published in the *Cornhill Magazine*, as follows:—
>
> | | |
> |---|---|
> | George the First | July, 1860. |
> | George the Second | Aug. 1860. |
> | George the Third | Sept. 1860. |
> | George the Fourth | Oct. 1860. |
>
> Vol. ii., pp. 1-20, 175-191, 257-277, 385-406.

137

THE ADVENTURES OF PHILIP ON HIS WAY THROUGH THE WORLD; SHEWING WHO ROBBED HIM, WHO HELPED HIM, AND WHO PASSED HIM BY. BY W. M. THACKERAY. In Three Volumes, pp. 329, 304, 301.—London: Smith, Elder, and Co., 65, Cornhill. 1862.

Originally published in instalments, and with illustrations, in the *Cornhill Magazine*, commencing the third volume in January, 1861. and ending in August, 1862 (vol. vi., p. 240).

The illustrations do not appear in the three-volume edition of the book, which has a Dedication to "M. J. Higgins," dated "Kensington, July, 1862."

138

ROUNDABOUT PAPERS, ETC.

These papers originally appeared in the *Cornhill Magazine*, as follows :

No. 1. On a Lazy, Idle Boy.—January, 1860 (vol. i., pp. 124-128).

No. 2. On Two Children in Black.—March, 1860 (vol. i., pp. 380-384).

No. 3. On Ribbons.—May, 1860 (vol. i., pp. 631-640).

No. 4. On some late Great Victories.—June, 1860 (vol. i., pp. 755-760).

No. 5. Thorns in the Cushion.—July, 1860 (vol. ii., pp. 122-128).

No. 6. On Screens in Dining-rooms.—August, 1860 (vol. ii., pp. 252-256).

No. 7. Tunbridge Toys.—September, 1860 (vol. ii., pp. 380-384).

No. 8. De Juventute.—October, 1860 (vol. ii., pp. 501-512).
A Roundabout Journey ; Notes of a Week's Holiday. —November, 1860 (vol. ii., pp. 623-640).

No. 9. On a Joke I once heard from the late Thomas Hood.—December, 1860 (vol. ii., pp. 752-760).

No. 10. Round about the Christmas Tree.—February, 1861 (vol. iii., pp. 250-256).

No. 11. On a Chalk-mark on the Door.—April, 1861 (vol. iii., pp. 504-512).

No. 12. On Being Found Out.—May, 1861 (vol. iii., pp. 636-640).

No. 13. On a Hundred Years Hence.—June, 1861 (vol. iii., pp. 755-760).

No. 14. Small-Beer Chronicle.—July, 1861 (vol. iv., pp. 122-128).

No. 15. Ogres.—August, 1861 (vol. iv., pp. 251-256).

No. 16. On Two Roundabout Papers which I intended to write.—September, 1861 (vol. iv., pp. 377-384).

E

No. 17. A Mississippi Bubble.—December, 1861 (vol. iv., pp. 755-760).

No. 18. On Lett's's Diary.—January, 1862 (vol. v., pp. 122-128).

No. 19. On Half-a-Loaf. A Letter to Messrs. Broadway, Battery and Co., of New York, Bankers.—February, 1862 (vol. v. pp. 250-256).

Nos. 20 to 22. The Notch on the Axe. A Story à la Mode. In Three Parts.—April,* May and June, 1862 (vol. v., pp. 508-512, 634-640, 754-760).

No. 23. De Finibus.—August, 1862 (vol. vi., pp. 282-288).

No. 24. On a Peal of Bells.—September, 1862 (vol. vi., pp. 425-432).

No. 25. On a Pear-Tree.—November, 1862 (vol. vi., pp. 715-720).

No. 26. Dessein's. December, 1862 (vol. vi., pp. 771-779).

No. 27. On Some Carp at Sans Souci. January, 1863 (vol. vii., pp. 126-131).

No. 28. Autour de mon Chapeau.—February, 1863 (vol. vii., pp. 260-267 .

On Alexandrines. A Letter to some Country Cousins. April, 1863 (vol. vii., pp. 546-552).

On a Medal of George the Fourth.—August, 1863 (vol. viii., pp. 250-256).

"Strange to say, on Club paper."—November, 1863 (vol. viii., pp. 636-640).

139

Denis Duval. By W. M. Thackeray.—London : Smith, Elder, and Co. 1867, pp. 275.

Denis Duval originally appeared in instalments in the *Cornhill Magazine*, of March, April, May and June, 1864, with illustrations (vol. ix., pp. 257-291, 385-409, 513-536, 641-665).

* On the reverse of the title of the number of the *Cornhill Magazine* for April, 1862, is a valedictory address of the Editor "To Contributors and Correspondents," on resigning his post, dated "March 18, 1862," and signed "W. M. T."

140

Mrs. Katherine's Lantern. (Written by W. M. Thackeray in a Lady's Album).—Printed in the *Cornhill Magazine*, January, 1867 (vol. xv., pp. 117-118).

141

The Anglers. By the late W. M. Thackeray, Esq. Seven stanzas of eight lines each.—Printed in *The Princess Alexandra Gift Book, edited by John Sherer*. London : Hamilton, Adams, and Co. 1868, pp. 22-23.

142

THE ORPHAN OF PIMLICO, AND OTHER SKETCHES, FRAGMENTS AND DRAWINGS. BY WILLIAM MAKEPEACE THACKERAY. With some Notes by Anne Isabella Thackeray. London : Smith, Elder, and Co. 1876 ; 4to, pages unnumbered.

Prefixed is a portrait of the author, "copied by Mr. Thackeray from a drawing by D. Maclise about 1840." The Preface (signed "A. I. T.") is dated "London, November 20, 1875."

143

Etchings by the late William Makepeace Thackeray while at Cambridge, illustrative of University Life, etc.   Now first published from the Original Plates. London : H. Sotheran and Co., Piccadilly.   1878.

List of Subjects :   1. Departure for Cambridge ; 2. Arrival from Cambridge ; 3. Worldly Study ; 4. Imposition ; 5. First Term ; 6. Second Term ; 7. Work Within ; 8. Pleasure Without ; 9. Collera Morbus ; 10. Scene from the Deluge ; 11. Ah, Mr. Goldfinch !

THACKERAYANA.

SKETCHES AND CARICATURES.

1

CHARLES IX. firing at the Huguenots out of the windows of the Louvre. Sketched on the blank portion of the yellow paper cover of a French drama.—Facsimiled in *The Recollections and Reflections of J. R. Planché.* London : Tinsley Brothers, 1872, vol. i., to face p. 171.

2

Signor Balfi. Sketch made in Mr. Planché's box during the performance of Balfe's opera, "The Siege of Rochelle," 16th November, 1835.—Facsimiled in Planché's *Recollections and Reflections,* vol. i., p. 241.

3

Note addressed to Planché, and signed " W. M. Thackeray," dated " 13, Great Coram-street, Brunswick-square," with pen-and-ink sketch of the State visit of the Queen and Prince Albert to Covent

Garden Theatre, 1840.—Facsimiled in Planché's
Recollections and Reflections, vol. ii., p. 40.

4

The Gamblers. A Sketch.—Facsimiled in *The Autographic Mirror*, No. 3, March 15, 1864 (vol. i.,
p. 27).

5

Note dated " 36, Onslow-square, 26th March, 1855,"
and signed " W. M. Thackeray."—Facsimiled in
The Autographic Mirror, No. 3, March 15, 1864,
p. 27.

6

Caricature Sketch of himself seated, writing on the
banks of the Nile, sketched on the first page of a
copy of " Cornhill to Cairo," presented to his friend,
William Bevan, and two letters, dated " 36, Onslow-
square, Brompton, February 21, 1855,"—one commencing, " My dear W. B." [William Bevan], and
the other, "My dear S."; both signed " W. M.
Thackeray."—The sketch and the two letters facsimiled in *The Autographic Mirror*, No. 17 (October
1, 1864), vol. ii., p. 139.

7

Thackeray's Writings.—*Edinburgh Review*, January,
1848 (vol. lxxxvii., pp. 46-67).

8

"Esmond." Essays by the late George Brimley,
M.A. Cambridge: Macmillan & Co., 1858, pp.
258-269.

Reprinted from the *Spectator* of November 6, 1852.

9

Essay on the Newcomes.—*Oxford and Cambridge
Magazine*. London: Bell & Daldy, 1856, pp.
50-61.
Thackeray and Currer Bell.—*Oxford and Cambridge
Magazine*, 1856, pp. 323-335.

10

THE MODERN NOVEL.—Dickens, Bulwer, Thackeray.
*Essays in Biography and Criticism by Peter Bayne,
M.A. First Series.* Boston: Gould and Lincoln,
1857, pp. 363-392.

11

William Makepeace Thackeray.—Printed in *Novels and Novelists from Elizabeth to Victoria.* By J. Cordy Jeaffreson. London: Hurst and Blackett, 1858, vol. ii., pp. 262-281.

Forming the thirteenth chapter of the second volume.

12

British Novelists and their Styles: being a Critical Sketch of the History of British Prose Fiction. By David Masson, M.A. Cambridge: Macmillan and Co., 1859.

Pages 233-253 are devoted to a consideration of Dickens and Thackeray.

13

Thackeray.—*Calcutta Review*, December, 1861 (vol. xxxvii., pp. 245-280).

14

William Makepeace Thackeray. With portrait from a photograph by Herbert Watkins.—*Illustrated London News*, January 9, 1864.

A memorial notice (signed "S. B."), written by the late Mr. Shirley Brooks.

15

In Memoriam. By Charles Dickens.

Historical Contrast, May, 1701; December, 1863 (Dryden and Thackeray), by Lord Houghton, signed "Hn."

W. M. Thackeray. By Anthony Trollope.

Cornhill Magazine, February, 1864 (vol. ix., pp. 129-137).

16

Thackeray.—*North British Review*, February, 1864 (vol. xl., pp. 210-265).

This article contains a printed version of *The Three Sailors*, different from those previously enumerated (p. 254), and fac-simile of a drawing by Thackeray representing Dr. Johnson and Goldsmith passing the shop of Filby, the tailor, with a street-boy and his little sister stepping out in mimicry of the two.

17

The National Shakespeare Committee and the late Mr. Thackeray. London: Joseph Clayton, 265, Strand, [1864], pp. 23.

18

THACKERAY, THE HUMOURIST AND THE MAN OF LETTERS. THE STORY OF HIS LIFE, including a

Selection from his Characteristic Speeches, now for the first time gathered together. By Theodore Taylor, Esq. With photograph from life by Ernest Edwards, B.A., and original illustrations. London : John Camden Hotten, Piccadilly, 1864, pp. vii. 223.

19

Footprints on the Road. By Charles Kent, Barrister-at-law. London : Chapman and Hall, 1864.

A chapter on " W. M. Thackeray, the Satirist-humourist," occupies pp. 370-407.

20

Haud Immemor : A Few Personal Recollections of Mr. Thackeray in Philadelphia. (Privately printed.) William P. Kildare, 422, Walnut-street, 1864, 8vo, pp. 31.

Contains six letters from W. M. Thackeray to W. B. Reed, dated—

1. Mr. Anderson's Music Store, Penn's Avenue, Friday.
2. Neufchatel, Switzerland, July 21, 1853.
3. 36, Onslow-square, Brompton, November 8, 1854.
4. Baltimore, January 16, 1856.
5. April 24, 1856.
6. Maurigy's Hotel, 1, Regent-street, Waterloo-place, April 2, 1859.

And a letter to Clement C. Biddle, dated Girard House (Philadelphia), January 23, 1853, and signed " W. M. Thackeray."

21

William Makepeace Thackeray. By one who knew him (Bayard Taylor).—Printed in *The Atlantic Monthly*, March, 1864 (vol. xiii., pp. 371-379).

22

A Brief Memoir of the late Mr. Thackeray. By James Hannay. (Reprinted from the *Edinburgh Courant*.) Edinburgh : Oliver and Boyd ; London : Simpkin, Marshall and Co., 1864, pp. 31.

23

Studies on Thackeray. By James Hannay. London : Routledge and Sons, *n.d.*, pp. 107.

With vignette portrait of Thackeray on title. The little work is divided into four chapters : " Thackeray as a Novelist," " Thackeray as a Humourist and Satirist," "Thackeray as a Critic and Essayist," "Thackeray as a Poet."

24

A Memorial of Thackeray's School-days. (Signed J. F. B.)—*Cornhill Magazine*, January, 1865 (vol. xi., pp. 118-128).

With five sketches by Thackeray.

25

Yesterdays with Authors. By James T. Fields. London : Sampson Low, 1872.

The chapter on Thackeray occupies pp. 11-37.

26

The Best of all Good Company. By Blanchard Jerrold. A Day with W. M. Thackeray. With facsimile page of extract from MS. letter. London : Houlston and Sons, Paternoster-buildings, 1872, 8vo. (numbered pp. 315-392).

27

Bric-a-Brac Series.—Anecdote Biographies of Thackeray and Dickens. Edited by Richard Henry Stoddard. New York : Scribner, Armstrong and Co., 1874.

The biography of Thackeray occupies the first 196 pages of the volume. A facsimile is given of one of his letters, with Sketch.

28

THACKERAYANA : Notes and Anecdotes illustrated by nearly six hundred sketches. By William Make-

peace Thackeray, depicting humorous incidents in
his school life, and favourite scenes and characters
in the books of his every-day reading. London:
Chatto and Windus, Piccadilly, 1875, pp. xx. 492.

Compiled by Mr. Joseph Grego.

29

Thackeray and Leech.—*Forty Years' Recollections of
Life, Literature and Public Affairs, from* 1830 *to* 1870.
By Charles Mackay, L.L.D. London: Chapman
and Hall, 1877, vol. ii., pp. 294-304.

30

An Essay on the Writings of W. M. Thackeray. By
Leslie Stephen. Printed in the twenty-fourth and
concluding volume of the Works of W. M. Thackeray. London: Smith, Elder and Co., 1879, pp.
313-378.

With two leaves of facsimile of autograph letter of W. M. T.
to Mr. Smith, dated "Sat. 29 Oct.," and Postscript to Roundabout Paper, dated "Dec. 16" (1861).

31

Thackeray. By Anthony Trollope. London: Macmillan and Co., 1879, pp. vi. 210.

In Nine Chapters. One of the series of "English Men of
Letters. Edited by John Morley."

32

Studies of English Authors. By Peter Bayne, M.A., LL.D.—W. M. Thackeray.—Printed in *The Literary World*, 1879-1880.

Commencing in the number for September 12, 1879, and continued weekly until March 19, 1880.

33

Great Novelists: Scott, Thackeray, Dickens, Lytton. By James Crabb Watt. Edinburgh: Macniven and Wallace, 1880.

The chapter on Thackeray occupies pp. 97-159.

34

Stray Moments with Thackeray: his humour, satire, and characters. Being Selections from his Writings, prefaced with a few Biographical Notes. By William H. Rideing. New York: D. Appleton and Co., 1880, pp. 192.

This little book forms one of "Appletons' New Handy-Volume Series."

THE END.

BILLING AND SONS, PRINTERS AND ELECTROTYPERS, GUILDFORD.

UNIFORM WITH THE BIBLIOGRAPHY OF THACKERAY.

In French grey wrapper, 5s.; or in cloth 6s., post free.

The Bibliography of Dickens.

A Bibliographical List of the Published Writings in Prose and Verse of CHARLES DICKENS, from 1834 to 1880, including his Letters and Speeches.

OPINIONS OF THE PRESS.

" Another of the works of reference, so invaluable to the student and bookworm. The work bears evidence of the careful manner in which it has been compiled, and must be a necessary item in future of all admirers of our greatest modern English humourist."—*The Pen.*

" It will be of especial interest and value to at least three important classes—the admiring readers of the great fictionist : the students who are anxious to trace the unfoldings of his genius and the growth of his power ; and the bibliographer proper or collector."—*The Scotsman.*

" A most laboriously compiled and minute bibliography."—*Bookseller.*

" Complete and in many respects curious."—*Daily News*

" This little work will be prized by all who admire the genius of Dickens, and desire to be comprehensively acquainted with his books, magazine contributions, speeches and letters."—*Literary World.*

" Singularly exhaustive and lucidly arranged."—*Illustrated London News.*

www.ingramcontent.com/pod-product-compliance
Lightning Source LLC
Chambersburg PA
CBHW021225260626
47172CB00002B/615